YOUR FAVOURITE
BEDTIME
STORIES
by Uncle Arthur
2

Illustrations by Annette Agard

ISBN 0-904748-71-5
5-vol. set 0-904748-75-8

Printed and published by
The Stanborough Press Ltd.
Alma Park, Grantham, Lincs., NG31 9SL
England

CONTENTS

Penny's 'sharing box'

I'm not quite sure who thought of it first, but I believe it was Penny. Anyway, it was a very beautiful idea.

Just before Christmas somebody said, 'This year, why don't we all give something to someone *outside* the family — someone who cannot possibly give a present in return?'

The idea caught fire. Pretty soon Penny put a big cardboard box in the middle of the dining-room floor. 'Let's make this our SHARING BOX,' she said. 'If anyone feels like giving a toy, or anything else, just drop it in here.'

Penny was first, bringing a doll she liked very much. With a tender goodbye she put it in the box. Gordon walked up next with his Teddy bear. Then came Sheena with her new box of paints.

Mother looked on in wonder, for she knew Sheena loved that box of paints very dearly.

Daddy put in a shirt he didn't like and a couple of pairs of shoes he thought were not too comfortable. The children said that wasn't fair; he should give something he really valued. Daddy was 'on the spot' for a while, until he remembered some new golf balls he had up-stairs. These, the children agreed, were a noble sacrifice.

Mother found two or three dresses, a couple of pretty petticoats, and a beautiful coloured scarf the children loved to see her wear.

'Oh, not that, Mummy!' said Sheena.

'Why not?' said Mother. 'Aren't we all trying to share our treasures with others today?'

Then the children started again. They looked in the toy cupboard more carefully. Out came games of one kind and another, and wind-up toys of all sorts. Sheena brought her woolly kitten, Gordon his Red Indian cap with the feathers in it, and Penny the crowning gift of all — the beautiful pencil box she treasured above everything else.

'Oh, not that,' said Mother.

'It's all right,' said Penny bravely. 'I would like to give it.'

'God bless you!' said Mother fondly, while Daddy turned his head away.

Gradually the sharing box was filled. Nobody grumbled, nor did anyone shed a tear. It was like having a Christmas tree *in reverse*: for everybody was giving without any thought of getting something in return.

Then Mother said, 'Now we must find people to whom we can give all these things. Let's all gather round the table and make a list of those who would be made happy by receiving them.'

'Bobbie Thompson would like my Teddy bear,' said Gordon. 'I'm sure he hasn't got one.'

'And Susan ought to have my paint box,' said Sheena. 'Her parents could never buy her one like that.'

'Old Tom Simmons will be glad of my golf balls,' said Daddy.

'And I'd like Kirsty Dawson to have my pencil box,' said Penny. 'I heard her say she would love one like that.'

And so it went on and on until every gift had been labelled for somebody who would be glad to receive it.

Then came the joy of wrapping the gifts and putting a little note inside, 'With Love From the Sharing Box.' Now followed the final happiness of delivering them.

Yet even that happiness wasn't 'final'. For happiness that comes from sharing never does come to an end. It goes on growing and spreading for ever.

The Christmas that Penny started her 'Sharing Box' idea was the happiest that the family had ever known.

Didn't Jesus say, 'It is more blessed to give than to receive'?

The parrot tries to escape

Brian and Jemma were playing in the sand-pit having a great old time together, when they noticed Mother coming towards them.

They looked up and began to stare. Not at Mother, but at what was perched on her shoulder.

It was Beauty, their pet parrot.

'Mummy,' they cried. 'You've brought Beauty out with you. Aren't you afraid he'll fly away?'

'Oh, I forgot!' said Mother. 'He was on my shoulder in the house and I've come out with him. I should have put him back in his cage.'

Mummy made a gentle grab for Beauty, but he hopped on to the top of her head. She made another grab, but missed again. He just didn't want to be caught. A moment later he spread his wings and took off, away up in the air.

'He's gone!' cried Brian.

'You shouldn't have brought him out,' said Jemma.

'I'm sorry, you two, but there's nothing we can do about it. Maybe he'll fly back on my shoulder again.'

But Beauty didn't fly back on to Mother's shoulder. He was too happy to be free. Away and away he went, until he was right out of sight.

Then the children felt very sad. So did Mother.

'The other birds will kill him,' said Brian.

'He won't have any nice cage to sleep in tonight,' said Jemma.

'Maybe we should pray and ask Jesus to look after him,' said Brian.

'I think we should,' said Mother. 'The Bible says that Jesus watches over every sparrow, so I feel sure He's interested in parrots too.'

Right then and there they knelt in the sand-pit and all three prayed that the Friend of sparrows would bring back their parrot.

But nothing happened. There wasn't even a flash of a blue wing to tell where Beauty had gone.

Mother went inside, and Brian and Jemma started to search for their precious pet.

After two hours or so, Brian was about ready to give up, but Jemma said, 'Let's pray again, and see what happens.'

'All right,' said Brian. 'Let's.'

So they went back to the sand-pit, knelt down again and prayed that Jesus would help them find their bird.

Then they started to search some more, round and round, up the hill and down the hill, into the bushes and out again. Still there was no sign of Beauty.

Another hour passed and Brian was getting very tired and discouraged.

'I'm afraid he's gone for good,' he said. 'Let's go inside.'

'Not yet,' said Jemma. 'Let's pray some more.'

'OK,' said Brian. 'But it doesn't seem to help much.'

'It might this time,' said Jemma.

So they knelt together in the sand-pit yet again.

'Dear Friend of the sparrows,' said Jemma very, very earnestly, 'please make Beauty come back home before night-time so he won't have to stay out in the dark.'

'Amen,' said Brian.

Then they got up off their knees and looked around again.

Suddenly Jemma let out a screech of delight.

'Look! Brian! See! There he is! Walking up the hill in the grass!'

'You're right!' cried Brian. 'It *is* Beauty.'

They ran towards the bird. Beauty flapped his wings, rose into the air, and landed on Jemma's shoulder.

'Mummy, Mummy!' they cried, running indoors. 'Look! Beauty has come home!'

Mother was as pleased as they were. Together they knelt on the kitchen floor and thanked the Lord for His loving care for parrots as well as sparrows, and for the wonderful way He answers children's prayers.

Kenny and the car

Kenny loved to go riding with his big brother Karl. It was always lots of fun.

You see, Karl was old enough to have a driving licence, and sometimes Daddy let him borrow his car so that he and Kenny could go for a ride in the country.

Daddy thought Karl was a very good driver, and he told his friends so. Little did he know what went on when he wasn't there.

The trouble was that when Karl had Kenny with him, he liked to show off. He would try to race other cars on the road, and whenever he came to a sharp corner he would make the tyres squeal just so he could hear Kenny scream.

That sort of driving, of course, always leads to trouble. Sooner or later a young person who drives that way is bound to have an accident. It's just a matter of time till it happens.

One day it happened to Karl. He had passed the top of a steep hill — travelling much too fast — and was just starting to go down the other side when something went wrong with his brakes. He tried to go into a lower gear, but couldn't because the car was moving too fast. Again and again he stabbed his right foot on the brake pedal — but nothing happened.

As best he could, Karl steered the car round one sharp bend after another. But as the speed increased he felt sure he couldn't get to the bottom in safety.

Very frightened, he began to pray out loud.

'Dear God,' he cried, 'Get me out of this! Don't let me wreck Dad's car!'

But he should have prayed that way before he started to take foolish risks.

The next bend did it. He couldn't turn the wheels in time. The car ran up the bank, turned over, and rolled back on to the road with a crash.

Unhurt, Karl scrambled out and began to drag Kenny after him. Kenny's right hand had been cut by a piece of broken glass, and Karl bound it up with his handkerchief.

White-faced and worried, the two boys stood looking at the car.

What a sight it was!

'Whatever will Daddy say?' said Kenny.

'He'll never let me drive again,' said Karl.

'How shall we ever get home?' asked Kenny.

'I don't know,' said Karl. 'I don't suppose anybody comes over this lonely road at this time of day. Somehow we'll have to get the car turned over so that we can drive home.'

'Could *you* turn it over?'

'Oh, no,' said Karl. 'That car weighs at least half a ton, and I couldn't lift that.'

'Not if *I* helped you?'

Karl smiled.

'We could try,' pleaded Kenny.

'All right then,' said Karl, knowing it was useless.

They tried, but the car wouldn't budge.

'I'm afraid we're stuck here for the night,' said Karl. 'Dad must be awfully worried by now. He'll never guess where we are.'

'Karl,' said Kenny.

'What?'

'I heard you praying in the car.'

'What of it?'

'Maybe if you told God you were sorry for what you've done, He might help us.'

'Help us, how?'

'Help us turn the car over.'

'Don't be silly.'

'It's worth trying. Are you sorry?'

'Of course I am.'

'Then tell God and ask Him for help.'

'All right,' said Karl.

On the steep hillside the two boys knelt in prayer, Karl telling God how sorry he was that he had been such a bad and foolish boy, and asking for forgiveness. Then he asked God to help them turn the car over.

In the distance they heard the sound of a car's engine. Another car was approaching.

Karl's first fear was that this car might run into their car. Standing in the road he waved his arms to attract the attention of the other driver.

The car slowed down. The driver wound down his

window. 'In trouble, boys?' he asked. 'Silly question. I can see you are. Anything I can do?'

That was when Karl and Kenny explained that they needed help pushing the car back on to its four wheels.

'Come on lads!' the driver shouted to three burly sons who were with him in his car. And all four big men jumped out and went to the aid of Karl and Kenny. Without Karl and Kenny lifting a finger, the four burly men soon had their car the right way up again.

After thanking the four strong men very enthusiastically, Karl started the engine, put the car into a low gear and, slowly, very slowly, drove safely home.

That day he had learned some lessons about driving. He had also learned another lesson: because of His love and His grace, God helps us out of difficulties that we have created for ourselves — when we ask Him.

Lakeside adventure

It was almost midnight and still they had not found the place where Daddy had planned to camp.

As the headlights shone around one corner after another Daddy kept saying, 'It's pretty close now; maybe just around the next corner.'

But it wasn't. All the time they were climbing higher and higher up the mountain.

Mother was getting more and more worried, because she felt that Beverley and Blossom should have been in bed fast asleep hours ago.

'Surely it can't be much further,' she said. 'Look, there's the lake down there. This must be the place.'

'You're right! You're right!' said Dad. 'That's the lake I was looking for. The camp can't be far away now. I think I'll leave you and the children in the car while I walk up the hill and see if I can find it.'

'Don't be long.'

'I won't,' said Dad.

When Daddy had gone Mother stepped out of the car to stretch her legs.

Suddenly in the darkness she had a dreadful feeling that the car was moving backwards. She put her hand on it.

Yes! It was slipping! She tried to get in it again to reach the brake, but she couldn't — the car was gathering speed by now. . . .

She called to Beverley to climb over to the front seat and step on the brake pedal, but that didn't help. The car kept moving.

Mother then grabbed the front bumper and tried to hold the car back. For a moment this seemed to help, but the car was too heavy for her and she soon felt herself being dragged downhill.

With gradually increasing speed the car moved nearer and nearer to the edge of the road, beyond which the hill dropped steeply into the deep, dark waters of the lake.

'Please, dear Jesus!' she cried aloud. 'Don't let it go over the edge!'

But it went over the edge. First one wheel, then another.

A moment later the front wheels followed the back wheels and the car was plunging headlong down, down, down towards the lake!

Did Mother let go? She did not. 'If my children are going to drown, I'll go with them,' she said to herself, as, holding on frantically to the bumper, she was dragged down the rocky slope.

The dark water now seemed to be leaping up at her out of the blackness of the night.

Beverley and Blossom, sensing their dreadful danger, were crying at the top of their voices, while Mother was crying aloud, 'Jesus, save my children!'

Suddenly there was a great bump and the car came to a standstill — right at the water's edge.

An old tree stump had stopped its headlong fall, just in time.

Beverley and Blossom told me of that awful night and, believe me, they love their mother! As long as they live they will never forget how she hung on to that bumper all the way down the hill and was willing to die with them if need be.

How wonderful is mother love! Did you ever stop to think that your mother would be willing to do the same for you? Of course she would! Why not show *her* a little bit of love right now?

They forgot his birthday

Tomorrow was Kevin's birthday. He was going to be 7! In a quiet sort of way he was very excited.

He went to bed early. Somebody had told him that his birthday would last longer if he went to bed early. By the end of his bed was that big empty chair. In the morning he would wake up and find it piled high with presents.

But when he woke up something was wrong.

The big chair was empty.

'Ah, well,' said Kevin to himself, 'my birthday present must be so big they couldn't get it upstairs.'

He could hear Mum and Dad, and his brothers and sisters downstairs. Quickly he put on his clothes and went down.

To his surprise Kevin found the family half way through breakfast.

There were no presents.

In fact, no one even wished him a happy birthday!

Kevin wanted to cry. But no one noticed. When the postman arrived there were no cards. Not even one from Grandma.

He went off to school very miserable. He was miserable all day then, just one hour from home time, Kevin had a happy thought. Maybe they had all been pretending at breakfast. Maybe when he arrived home he would find a party such as never was — with stacks of presents. They were planning a surprise.

Kevin *was* in for a surprise.

When he arrived home there was no sign of a birthday party. Mum was just as usual.

Teatime came and went.

No party. No presents.

There was an empty feeling inside Kevin. He wanted to cry, but couldn't.

The awful truth sank in: *Everyone had forgotten his birthday!*

It was about this point that Kevin woke up.

It was still dark.

He'd had a horrible dream.

But suddenly he felt happy again. If it was still dark, his birthday hadn't even started yet. . . .

Jesus was not born on 25 December. But everyone has chosen to celebrate His birthday on that date.

Lots of parties are held. But Jesus is not invited along.

Lots of presents are given. But how many think of giving a present to Jesus?

Do you think Jesus feels hurt when He is forgotten on His own birthday, as Kevin did when he thought he was forgotten on his?

What can you give Jesus on His birthday?

An old carol says:

   'What can I give Him, poor as I am?

    If I were a shepherd I would give a lamb;

If I were a wise man I would do my part;
Yet what can *I* give Him? Give Him my heart.'

Roger's rocket

Roger was working with a long piece of pipe in the garage as Daddy drove in.

'What's happening now?' asked Daddy cheerily as he got out of the car.

'I'm making a rocket,' said Roger. 'It should go up about 500 feet when I set it off.'

'But what do you know about rockets?' asked Daddy.

'Oh, lots,' said Roger confidently. 'Several of us boys have formed a rocket club. We learned a lot about rockets in chemistry class and Tommy Mason says he knows where he can get the fuel. So we're all making rockets and one day we'll shoot them up into the sky.'

'Making rockets can be very dangerous,' said Daddy.

'Not if you're careful,' said Roger.

'Is your teacher going to be with you when you load and fire them?'

'Oh, no,' said Roger. 'We don't want any teachers around. We're going to do it all by ourselves.'

'I don't like it,' said Daddy seriously. 'When you're playing with explosives you need all the experience you can get.'

'Oh, don't be old fashioned, Daddy,' said Roger. 'Everybody's making rockets these days.'

'It's not old fashioned to use a bit of common sense,' said Daddy as he went into the house. 'And, remember, keep away from the things when you fire them. They sometimes explode.'

But Roger didn't want any advice just then. He knew everything.

Some days later he went off to the secret meeting place of his club, some distance out of town. Several of the boys arrived with home-made rockets of various shapes and sizes. Together they filled them with the explosives Tommy Mason had provided. Then they prepared to fire them.

Tommy took charge.

'I'll send mine up first,' he said. 'The rest of you get behind that rock and stay there till you see it rise. Something just might go wrong.'

He lit the fuse of his rocket and dashed for cover.

There was a sizzling roar and the rocket sped skyward — 100, 200, maybe 300 feet.

'Jolly good!' shouted the rest, and Tommy glowed with pride.

The next one went up twenty feet or so, then fell to the ground and sputtered out. The third never rose at all. Only two or three others were really successful.

Then it came to Roger's turn.

'Mine's going to the moon!' he bragged. 'Look out everybody! I'm going to light my fuse!'

He lit it and stood watching.

'Get behind the rock!' yelled Tommy. 'Haven't you got any sense?'

The warning came too late.

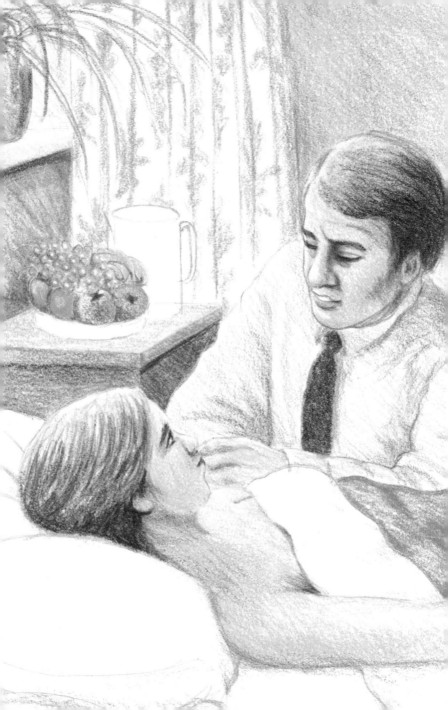

Suddenly there was a loud bang as the rocket exploded into tiny fragments.

When Roger woke he was in hospital. Daddy was sitting beside his bed.

'That was a close shave, son,' Daddy was saying.

'It was,' murmured Roger. 'You were so right, Daddy. I should have been more careful. Next time I'll have more sense, more common sense, just as you said.'

He never said a wiser word.

Heidi's unexpected present

It was a week before Christmas. Eight-year-old Heidi and her brother Marcus were shopping with Mother.

Such a happy time they were having! It was great fun buying presents for everybody, and spending all the money they had been saving up for the past few months.

Heidi's arms were full of brown paper parcels. She had a present for Daddy, another for Marcus, and a very special one for Mother. Oh, yes, and still another for Aunt Jane, and a teeny-weeny one for cousin Mary, who was only six months old.

Mother had a lot of parcels too, and she was standing at the counter in the toy department buying one more present when the worst thing possible happened. Marcus disappeared!

Heidi was the first to notice he had gone.

'Mummy!' she called. 'Where's Marcus?'

Mother looked around anxiously.

'Marcus?' she said. 'Isn't he with you?'

'No! He just ran away. How shall we ever find him in this crowd of people?'

'Oh dear!' cried Mother. 'I can't leave here for a moment. I'm in the middle of paying a bill. You go and look for him.'

'But I'll drop my parcels,' said Heidi.

'Put them down here and I'll look after them.'

Hastily Heidi put her armful of parcels on a stack of books and hurried off in search of her baby brother.

'Marcus! Marcus!' she shouted as she dodged in and out of the shoppers as they stood in the aisles and crowded round the counter.

She felt pretty sure that Marcus would probably still be somewhere in the toy department, most likely looking at something that had caught his fancy earlier.

She was right. Turning a corner she saw him sitting in a 'spaceship', perfectly happy and without a thought that his mother and big sister were wondering where he was.

'Marcus!' cried Heidi. 'You shouldn't run away like this. Mummy is terribly worried about you.'

Taking him firmly by the hand, Heidi hurried back to Mother.

'Here he is,' she said. 'Now where are my parcels?'

'Over there,' said Mother, 'on that pile of books. Pick them up and we'll go home before Marcus gets into any more mischief.'

Heidi gathered up her parcels, tucking them as carefully as she could under her arm, and followed Mother and Marcus to the door and so to the bus and home.

When they got home Heidi put her shopping on the kitchen table. 'Look, Mummy! An extra present.'

'What do you mean?' asked Mother.

'Just look as this!' she cried, holding up a beautiful book of animal pictures.

'Did you buy that?' asked Mother.

'Oh, no,' said Heidi. 'I've never seen it before.'

'Then where did you get it?'

'I don't know. I just found it on the table.'

'Heidi,' said Mother seriously, 'you must have picked that up in the shop by mistake.'

'Maybe I did,' said Heidi. 'Mother, look at the book. It's lovely,' she said. 'And see the price! Just to think I brought home a book like that without knowing it!' said Heidi. 'I do hope nobody will think I stole it!'

'What do you think we should do about it?' asked Mother.

'Oh,' said Heidi at once, 'I'm sure Jesus would want me to send it back, wouldn't He?'

'Yes, indeed,' said Mother. 'And I'm glad you thought of that first. It would be nice if you would write a little note to the manager telling him how it happened. Then we'll wrap the book up carefully and send it back.'

'Maybe I should write the letter now while I'm thinking about it,' said Heidi.

'A good idea,' said Mother. 'While I prepare tea.'

So Heidi wrote her little note:

'Dear Mr. Manager, This afternoon when I was in your shop I picked up a book by mistake with my other parcels. I didn't find out about it till I got home. I'm very sorry. And because I didn't pay for it I'm sure

God would want me to send it back. So I'm sending it. With love from your little friend, Heidi.'

Mother read the note and said she thought it was very nice. Then she tucked it into the book, which she wrapped ready for posting.

A few days later, just before Christmas — and this is quite true — Heidi received a reply to her letter. The manager wrote to say how pleased he was to know there was such an honest little girl in town. And because she had sent the book back so promptly he was sending her a little present to show his appreciation.

When the gift arrived it proved to be a pair of beautiful red slippers. They were so lovely, and so unexpected, that Heidi could hardly believe her eyes. She put them on at once and danced all round the house in pure delight. Indeed, every time she put them on she felt a warm glow inside, she was so glad that she had done the right thing and sent that book back!

Lost at a picnic

'We're going for a picnic this afternoon,' said Mother.

'Good!' cried Julia.

'Oh boy!' said Trevor.

'Hurry up then,' said Daddy. 'Get ready!'

Soon they were off.

Arriving at the forest where they were to spend the afternoon, Trevor and Julia said they wanted to eat at once.

'I'm starving!' cried Trevor.

'Me, too!' said Julia.

So they found a nice spot where a big oak gave shelter from the sun. Then they all sat down while Mother unpacked the picnic basket.

Trevor was so hungry that he gobbled up his food in no time. So fast, in fact, that he wanted to eat Julia's too. But she wouldn't let him.

'All right,' said Trevor, 'if there's no more food, I'm going for a walk.'

'Great!' said Mother. 'But don't go too far.'

'I won't,' said Trevor.

But he did. He walked on and on through the forest until he didn't know where he was. As the sun went down he became very worried. He wanted to find Mummy and Daddy and Julia. But how? Which way should he take? Every tree looked like every other tree and there was no path that he could follow. Of course, he should have made marks on the trees as he walked, but he didn't. He forgot. Now he was lost.

He shouted and shouted, but no one answered.

'Mummy! Daddy! Julia!' he shouted at the top of his voice, but there was no reply.

What a long way he must have walked! Surely, he thought, they would be calling him by now. Yet he could hear nothing but the strange little noises of the forest.

It was getting darker now. Trevor started to cry. He was feeling very lonely and frightened. He had never stayed out all night in the open before. Would some wild animal come and eat him up?

Just then he spied a little log cabin.

Good! he thought. If somebody is living in this cabin he'll take me back to Mummy.

Trevor knocked on the cabin door.

But nobody answered. Then he pushed the door and, to his surprise, it opened. He went inside. The place was empty and bare. But at least it was shelter. He wouldn't have to stay out all night.

How dark it was now! How he wished Daddy would come — and Mummy and Julia! It was dreadful being without them.

Then he remembered something Mummy had told him one day. She had said that if ever he didn't know what to do he should ask Jesus to help him.

So he did. In that dark, bare little cabin in the forest Trevor prayed his first real prayer.

'Please help Daddy to find me!' he asked.

Then, very tired and very hungry, he lay on the floor and fell asleep.

Early next morning, as sunshine streamed through the window, he was awakened by shouts.

'Look in that cabin,' someone was saying. 'Maybe he's in there.'

Trevor rushed to the door and flung it open.

Outside in the clearing he saw Daddy and some other men who had been searching the forest all night.

'Daddy!' he screamed with delight as tears of joy rolled down his cheeks.

Soon he was home again with Mummy and Julia, who gave him the best and biggest meal he had ever eaten in all his life.

'Do you know something?' said Trevor afterwards. 'Do you know what happened in that cabin?'

'What?' said Mummy.

'I asked Jesus to help Daddy find me, and He did.'

'Of course!' said Mummy, tears shining in her eyes. 'Of course, darling! I know He did.'

Lee's secret

'I wish I could be a pirate!' said Lee. 'Everything is so dull, and I want to do something exciting.'

'Yes,' said Nicola, 'Let's find something to do.'

It was the school holidays. Term had been finished for about ten days, and the children were getting tired of their play things. They wanted something new.

'Of course, we can't be pirates,' said Nicola, 'because we should soon be taken to the police station.'

'Of course,' said Lee, 'but can't we think of something?'

'Let's think.'

So they thought and thought. Neither of them spoke for several minutes. Then Lee jumped to his feet.

'I've got it!' he cried. 'Let's call ourselves the "Surprise Packet Company". I'll be the president, and you, Nicola, well, you can be the secretary.'

'All right, Lee,' said Nicola, willing to do anything her big brother suggested. 'But what shall we do?'

'Do? Give people surprises!'

'What sort of surprises?'

'Oh, good ones, of course,' said Lee. 'We'll find people who need things done for them and then make them wonder how the things happened. I think we'll get lots of fun out of it.'

'So do I,' said Nicola. 'What shall we do first? Let's start soon.'

'All right. I'll make a list of things and then we can decide which to start with.'

Lee found a pencil and paper and made his list.

'Now,' he said solemnly, 'don't you go and tell anybody about what we are planning to do. It's just a secret between us two.'

'Of course,' said Nicola, 'as if I *would* tell!'

That same afternoon when Mother returned from town she just dropped into an armchair and stared. What a transformation! After dinner she had gone out hurriedly, leaving all the dirty dishes beside the sink. Now they had disappeared. The kitchen had been tidied up, everything was in its place, and the table was all set for tea. By the side of the open fire, instead of an empty coal-scuttle, there was a full one. And, yes, even the windows had been cleaned!

All was quiet and still. Nobody was about. What kind person could have done all this?

Lee and Nicola came in from the garden. Mother asked them if Aunty had called during the afternoon. Lee said No, he didn't think so, but it did look as though someone had been busy.

'Well,' said Mother, 'isn't it just lovely! I haven't any more work today. I wonder who did it all.'

Mother opened a letter she had found on the mat when coming in. It read:

'The ''Surprise Packet Company'' called this afternoon.'

'I wonder what that means,' said Mother.

'I wonder,' said Lee.

'Let's have tea,' said Nicola.

And they did.

Next morning two children might have been seen going down the street leading to the little bungalow of Mrs. O'Higgins, a poor, bedridden old soul for whom nobody seemed to care.

The boy, who was holding something carefully in his right hand, knocked gently upon the door. There was no answer. He peeped in at the window. Mrs. O'Higgins was fast asleep. Quietly opening the door, he walked in, followed by his sister. Tiptoeing across the room, the boy placed the parcel he was carrying on the table beside the bed and went out. The little girl was so excited that she fell over the doorstep.

'Nicola, be careful!' said the boy.

The noise had awakened the old lady. 'Who is that?' she called. But the door was shut, and the two children were scampering away as fast as their legs would carry them.

Mrs. O'Higgins picked up the parcel. It contained three eggs.

'What a mercy!' she said to herself. 'But who sent them?'

Looking at the wrapper, she read: 'With love from the "Surprise Packet Company".'

Geoff Morley, a school friend of Lee's, was ill with mumps. Of course, he had to stay indoors and was very miserable. From his bed he could just look out over a small patch of garden, surrounded by a high brick wall.

One afternoon he was gazing vacantly out of the window when all of a sudden he saw a square box topple over the garden wall and slide down to the ground, held by a stout string.

'Mother, quick!' he called. 'Look! What is that in the garden?'

Mother, surprised, fetched the parcel and Geoff opened it. Inside were four smaller parcels. One was labelled: 'Open on Monday'; the second, 'Open on Wednesday'; the third, 'Open on Friday'; the fourth 'Open on Sunday'.

As it was Monday, Geoff opened the first parcel. It was a box of paints. Just what he had been longing for! Inside the box were the words:

'With best wishes from the "Surprise Packet Company".'

'Whatever is that?' asked Geoff.

Nobody knew.

On one occasion the 'Surprise Packet Company' were caught out.

Lee and Nicola were paying a second visit to Mrs. O'Higgins. This time they had taken with them some flowers as well as eggs. As quiet as mice they crept in, placed their gifts on the table, and left.

The children were so anxious to get in and out without waking up the old lady that they didn't notice the gentleman sitting quietly in the next room. It was the doctor.

No sooner had the door closed behind the children

than he went across to the table and read the note:

'With love from the "Surprise Packet Company".'

'So this explains what the old lady has been talking about!' he said. 'And now I can understand what Geoff Morley told me yesterday.'

And this explains, too, how it came about that a few days later a letter arrived at the home of Lee and Nicola addressed to the 'Surprise Packet Company' and containing an invitation to tea at Dr. Brown's.

It was a wonderful tea that the children had at the doctor's, and there were two surprise packets there that made up for all that they had given away.

Of course, the children could not understand how the doctor had come to know about their secret, and he wouldn't say a word. It was all a delightful mystery. Lee and Nicola were as happy as children could be. Lee said that it was much better than being pirates.

The wrong way to do it

Two little girls had been having a serious quarrel, and both were very angry. It wasn't easy to discover what it was all about, but probably nothing in particular.

When the noise was at its height, and hair was being pulled and faces slapped, and very naughty things being said, Mother came on the scene.

'Quarrelling again!' she said. 'I'm ashamed of you both. And, Angela, I'm surprised at you for setting such a bad example to your little sister. Off to bed, both of you! You've both been up too long already. That's why you're both so cranky.'

Amid much grumbling and muttering as the two went upstairs, Mother followed them. As soon as they were in bed, she tucked them in and started to give them their goodnight kiss when she noticed that the sulky look was still on Angela's face.

'Angela,' she said, 'you mustn't go to sleep feeling like this. You must make friends with Julie. If anything were to happen to her in the night you'd never forgive yourself.'

Angela remained silent. She knew very well what she *ought* to do, but there was something inside her trying to keep her from doing it.

Mother thought it best not to say any more, and

tiptoed towards the door, where she stood and listened.

After a while she heard a rustling of the bedclothes and Angela's voice speaking.

'Julie,' she called across the bedroom, 'Mum says we've got to make up and be friends. She says I ought to be sorry, so I suppose I must be; but if you don't die tonight, you'll catch it in the morning for sure!'

Mother was horrified.

'Angela!' she cried, stepping back into the bedroom. 'How could you say such a terrible thing! That's not the way to be sorry. To be sorry, you must forgive and forget.'

'But she slapped my face . . .' began Angela.

'Perhaps she did, and it was very naughty of her, but what does Jesus say? Don't you remember? "If someone smites you on one cheek, turn to him the other also." That's what little Christian children are supposed to do. They mustn't fight.'

'But she's always pestering me, and dirtying my doll's clothes, and breaking my toys.'

'But she's your own little sister,' said Mother. 'And you must try to teach her. Have you forgotten, too, the part in the Bible where it says: "Love your enemies, bless those who curse you, do good to those who hate you, and pray for those who use you spitefully, and persecute you"? That's the way we are to treat those who seem to be unkind to us. We don't fight them. We love them.'

Angela grunted, and the sound seemed to come from down beneath her pillow somewhere.

'I think we should do what Jesus says and pray for her, don't you?' suggested Mother. 'Let's kneel down now; I think you must have forgotten your prayers tonight.'

Rather reluctantly Angela got out of bed, and they both knelt down together and said a prayer for little sister. Then they said, 'Our Father,' and when they came to 'Forgive us our trespasses,' Mother paused while Angela went on by herself.

'As we forgive those who trespass against us,' she said in a trembling little voice.

All of a sudden the meaning of the words seemed to come home to her. Getting up from her knees, she went over to Julie's bed and kissed the tear-stained face.

'I'm really sorry now,' she said. 'And I'm sure you won't die tonight, because I know some great games we can play together in the morning.'

The house by the river

Maggie lived in a little house by the side of a great river.

Maggie's house was part of a row of tiny houses which had seen better days. Some people said they were dangerous and should be pulled down. But Maggie didn't worry. She told her Sunday school pupils: 'I trust in God, no matter what.'

One terrible night the wind howled and the rain lashed down. Late, late into the night a strange wailing sound could be heard from the great river, the Firth of Forth. It was so loud that it woke many of the children up in the little town. One boy asked what it was and was told, 'It's a flood warning,' and he thought of his Sunday school teacher in her little house by the water's edge.

Next day he went to Sunday school. Before Maggie arrived the minister told the children the sad news.

The great Firth of Forth had burst its banks in the night. All the downstairs of Maggie's house had been flooded. Her carpets and curtains had been ruined. The pigsties at the nearby farm were completely under water. . . . Before the minister could say more, Maggie burst into the school room. What a sorry sight! All wet and wild, her overcoat torn. But she was excited and smiling. 'Praise God, we're all safe,' she said. 'And did you know that pigs can swim?'

Years passed. Most people moved away from the tiny houses by the great Firth of Forth. For some reason Maggie stayed on. Bad boys broke the windows of the other houses, but soon ran away when Maggie came after them.

One evening in summer the Sunday school children heard an alarm and the bells of a racing fire engine. A group of them ran after it. They saw the bad boys running in the other direction.

When they reached the tiny houses by the Firth of Forth the fire was almost over. Very little was left of Maggie's tiny house. There was Maggie out front with the firemen, watching smoke rising from the few remaining embers. On either side of where her house had been were two walls. Upstairs, in what had been Maggie's bedroom, the children saw a fireplace — but no floor! Maggie was pointing to the cupboard in the wall by the fireplace. 'Up there! Up there!' She shouted to the firemen.

'I'm not going up there!' said one fireman. 'In any case it will have been burned to a cinder.'

But Maggie insisted.

Carefully the fireman leaned his ladder against the bare wall. Slowly he climbed up it. When he reached the top he opened the door of the cupboard in the wall by the fireplace. He reached in. When he pulled his hand out he was holding Maggie's Bible. It was not burned, despite the fact that it had a box of matches on top of it!

Below, Maggie received it smiling.

'That's all that's left,' said the fireman.

'*That's* all I wanted,' said Maggie.

Not long after the fire, Maggie was given a brand new bungalow. The folk in the little town even gave her some more furniture.

'God is good,' she told her children in Sunday school.

'But', said a little boy from the back, 'would you still have trusted in Him if you hadn't got your Bible back?'

'Oh, yes,' said Maggie. 'I trust in God no matter what.'

Maggie told the class of a promise God made in Isaiah chapter 42 verses 2 and 3: 'When you go through deep waters and great trouble, I will be with you. When you go through rivers of difficulty, you will not drown! When you walk through the fire of oppression, you will not be burned up — the flames will not consume you. For I am the Lord your God, your Saviour.' (The Living Bible.)

'In other words,' said Maggie, 'when the hard times come, God will be with us — no matter what.'

Brave Christine

Many years ago a whole nation cheered for the actions of one little girl. The nation was Scotland, the girl's name was Christine, and it was no wonder everyone cheered for the brave thing that she did. You'll cheer too when you hear her story.

One day while playing outside her home she smelt smoke. At first she thought that someone had just burnt some food on the stove or something, but soon the smell became too strong for that.

Looking back at her own home she was startled to see her old grandfather staggering out of the front door, with smoke billowing behind him. Her house was on fire!

'Where are the children?' she yelled, rushing over to him.

'I don't know!' he gasped. 'I couldn't see them. There was too much smoke.'

'I'm going in to find them,' cried Christine, trying to push her way through the throng of neighbours who had already gathered at the door.

'You can't go in there!' they cried. 'You'll be suffocated. Wait for the fire brigade. It'll be here in a minute.'

But Christine had no intention of waiting, not with her precious brothers and sisters inside — and the new baby.

Breaking away from the neighbours, she ran around the house. All the windows were shut. She looked for a stick or something she could use to break the glass. She couldn't find anything. So she hammered at the window with her fist until the glass broke. Then she clambered inside.

The smoke was so thick that she could hardly see the furniture. So she got down near the floor and made her way as quickly as she could to the kitchen where she guessed the children would be.

They were there all right, and four of them were leaning over the baby to protect her!

'Quick!' she cried. 'Let me take the baby!'

She took the baby and put her over her shoulder. Then, grabbing the two smallest children, one in each hand, she struggled to the window, ordering the two older children to follow her. The heat scorched them, the smoke choked them, but, keeping near the floor, they finally made it to the window.

Meanwhile the firemen had arrived and were about to turn their hoses on the burning house. Spying the broken window, one of them peered inside. To his amazement he could dimly see through the smoke a girl with a baby on her shoulder, her arms around two other children, and two more behind. He could hardly believe his eyes. 'They're here!' he shouted, grabbing the baby, and helping the others out one by one. A sigh of relief ran through the crowd.

By this time Christine's hand was bleeding badly from

the broken glass, but she didn't mind. She had saved her whole family by her bravery and her calm good sense. No wonder all Scotland cheered!

Once too often

If there was one thing Daddy was very strict about it was the way children acted in a boat. He would never permit any fooling about. It was much too dangerous. Too many people had been drowned because of it. If anybody started to jump up and down or lean too far over the side, Daddy really told them what he thought.

One spring afternoon Daddy decided to go water-skiing. So he hitched his boat trailer to the car and set off for the lake, taking Mummy, Joy and Jeanette with him.

Mummy loved to water-ski, and she had the first turn. Daddy drove the boat at top speed around the lake, with Mummy riding along on the skis, while Joy and Jeanette enjoyed the thrill of the bumpy ride and the spray, and admiring Mummy's skill.

When Mummy got tired, Daddy towed her in near the shore. Then he jumped out of the boat and got ready to put on the skis as Mummy took them off.

Left alone in the boat, Joy and Jeanette began to play about.

'Sit down!' said Daddy. 'Remember what I told you. No fooling about in a boat.'

They sat down, but not for long. Joy couldn't sit still long anyway. She was too full of life and mischief.

Pretty soon she was up again, trying to make the boat rock from side to side.

'Joy!' cried Daddy. 'Stop it! If you do that again you will have to be punished.'

Joy sat down. But not for more than a minute or two. Pretty soon she was pushing one of the oars out over the side.

'Put that oar back!' roared Daddy. 'Just you wait till I get in that boat again.'

Joy sat very still for a few minutes. Then she crawled to the back of the boat where the engine was still gently purring, out of gear.

Daddy, still holding on to the boat with one hand, was reaching for the skis as Mummy passed them over to him. In a moment or two she would have been in the boat ready to give him a tow, but she didn't get there.

I really don't know how it happened. Neither does anybody else, but suddenly that boat took off at full speed.

Obviously Joy had something to do with it, but she never could remember just exactly what she did.

Anyhow, there was the boat shooting out into the lake, with Daddy holding on with one hand.

To put it mildly, he was not pleased.

'Turn that engine off!' he yelled.

Joy couldn't. She didn't know how. Finally Jeanette crawled down the boat to the back and turned the engine off. Daddy climbed aboard, started the engine again, turned the boat around and headed for the bank.

As they neared the shore Joy wished she was wearing

something thicker than a swimsuit. And she had good reason.

'This is once too often,' said Daddy, as his hand went up and down. 'Don't-you-ever-fool-about-in-a-boat-again!'

Joy had to sit in the car for the rest of the afternoon and watch the others enjoying the boat ride and the water skiing. But she learned her lesson and never played about in a boat again.